Dedicated to ALL.

"To get the full value of joy
you must have
Someone to divide it with."
—Mark Twain

Special thanks
to these folks:

Published by Roaring Brook Press
Roaring Brook Press is a division of Holtzbrinck Publishing Holdings Limited Partnership
120 Broadway, New York, NY 10271
mackids.com

Library of Congress Cataloging-in-Publication Data is available.
ISBN: 978-1-250-20848-4

Our books may be purchased in bulk for promotional, educational, or business use. Please contact your
local bookseller or the Macmillan Corporate and Premium Sales Department at (800) 221-7945 ext. 5442
or by email at MacmillanSpecialMarkets@macmillan.com.

First edition, 2020
Book design by Aram Kim
Printed in China by Toppan Leefung Printing Ltd., Dongguan City, Guangdong Province

1 3 5 7 9 10 8 6 4 2

THE TROUBLE with PENGUINS

rebecca jordan-glum

Roaring Brook Press

New York

On the day the penguin discovered the person, everything changed. The penguin had been waddling along in a most penguinish manner, minding its own penguin business . . .

until it wasn't.

"Oh, hello! I'm roasting marshmallows.
Would you like one?"

Of course the penguin would
like a marshmallow. (It liked
it very much, in fact!)

"Come on! I'll show you how."

The new friends roasted marshmallows
together by the little fire.

When it was time for the penguin
to go home, the person gave it a hug

and the very best roasting stick,

and they shared a warm goodbye.

Naturally, the other penguins were quite impressed
and wanted to roast marshmallows by the fire, too.

At first, they were all happy to share one little fire that gave off the most delightful warmth.

They found fun ways to pass the time when it wasn't their turn,

which everyone was happy doing . . .

until they weren't.

You see, the trouble with penguins is that they don't always like to share.

Before long, each wanted its own roasting
stick and its own campfire.

They built fire . . .

after fire . . .

after fire after fire
after fire after fire
after fire after fire
after after fire
after fire after fire
after fire after fire
after fire after fire
after fire after fire
after fire after fire
after fire after fire
after fire after fire

UNTIL...
SOMETHING
HAPPENED.

And just like that each penguin had its very own roasting stick, its very own fire, and, best of all, its very own island, which was wonderful . . .

until it wasn't.

It was lonely.

Now, everyone knows the trouble with penguins is that they aren't always good at admitting when they're wrong.

Thankfully, penguins are full of good intentions
and aren't half bad at learning from their mistakes.

"Would you like to share my fire with me?"

It liked it very much, in fact.

They all did.

And of course, nobody likes to be left out.

So they decided to give it another try . . .

and that was no trouble at all.